Hedgehogs

ISEULT MURPHY

Cover illustration by Phan Duy

Cover design and Interior illustrations by I Murphy

Version 07.22

ISBN: 9798842701285

Also By

For Helveticus and Athena

CONTENTS

CHAPTER 1

The field called to him. Harry knew he should have been concerned that all he could smell was the delicious aroma of the field. It wasn't normal, and it left him vulnerable having to rely on his other senses, but the odour was so alluring that it seemed to do something to his brain. It short circuited his desire for self-preservation, and he knew that should really bother him, but somehow, he didn't care.

Take the blurry shape wandering down the grass verge towards him for instance. He should be hiding under a bush or rolling into a ball rather than barrelling toward it. It looked too tall for a badger, but it could be a dog and a part of him warned him to be cautious. He didn't listen. He was already salivating with the prospect of the feast laid out for him in the field. He couldn't wait to get there and tuck in.

The shape resolved into the familiar dog fox, Roy, once Harry was within biting distance. He kept walking stolidly onward, but Roy put out his paw and stopped him.

"I wouldn't go that way if I were you."

Harry was usually so good natured, he surprised himself by snarling at Roy and nipping at the fox's paw to let him pass.

"Out of my way, I need to get to the field."

Roy pulled a face, wrinkled his muzzle and stuck out his tongue as if he'd eaten something that tasted funny.

"There's something wrong with that field. It smells bad. You should forage somewhere else tonight, spikey one."

Harry tried to push past, but Roy moved to block his way again.

"Can't you smell the glorious scent? Don't you just want to roll in it?"

Roy sneezed and pawed at his nose. Harry took the opportunity to move under the fox and continue up the side of the road towards the field.

"Be careful, little hog. There's something dangerous in the field. I have to get away from the smell and you should too, if you have any sense."

Harry licked his own nose. What did the fox know? The field's smell grew more enticing the nearer he drew to it. He noticed other hedgehogs hurrying along the road towards the field. He was surprised to see so many as he often went nights without seeing another of his kind, although he might smell them among the undergrowth. A young mother and her hoglets walked ahead of him. The little ones looked six weeks or older, almost ready to leave their mother's flanks. They played gently with each other as they followed their mother.

Harry would like to have a litter someday. He hoped he'd find a nice young hedgehog, maybe tonight would be the night in the field. He certainly would have plenty of opportunity. There were so many hogs gathering.

He crossed the verge and battled through the long grass further from the road. He heard worms moving in the damp soil of the ditch as he walked along the bottom, but he ignored them. The field had better, more succulent food for him. He would try his luck there.

Climbing out the other side of the ditch, he pushed his way through the hedge. The field was on the other side. He had never felt so excited in his life.

He had to pass the rabbit burrow to get to the field. Six young rabbits sat around the burrow opening. Harry was surprised so many rabbits had gathered in the open.

"Evening."

One young doe squealed and jumped in the air, flashing her white tail, which made the other rabbits roll around laughing.

"It's just another hedgehog, Speedy."

"Another one?" The doe drew her long ear through her paws. "There's hundreds out tonight."

"I don't mind." A scrawny buck lounged back on the grass, stretching out his powerful back legs. "The horrible smell of the field keeps all the predators away."

"How can you call it horrible? It is the most wonderful smell ever."

Harry was incensed.

"Oh, go join the other hedgehogs. You have lost your senses, the lot of you."

The rabbits laughed, and Harry hurried on. Rabbits were stupid anyway. What did they know? They were no better than foxes.

Still, at the back of his mind, Harry wondered if there was something in what they said. Why were all the hedgehogs congregating on the field? Why couldn't he resist the smell? What was going on?

Normally he loved sorting out puzzles, but the smell of the field brushed away all his qualms and questions until all he knew was the field.

It stretched before him now in the moonlight. Among the neat rows of vegetables, he saw hundreds of blurry hedgehog sized shapes moving jerkily. Slugs, beetles, earwigs and millipedes, Harry's favourites, lay unmoving around the base of the veg. It was a veritable hedgehog heaven. He didn't even have to forage, the food just lay there waiting to be eaten.

Harry paused on the headland before stepping onto the field and gorging himself on the creepy crawlies. Something was very wrong. A fine dust coated the earth around the vegetables, the source of the enticing smell. Harry didn't want to get it on his paws. Deep inside he screamed to turn around and leave before it was too late.

The field smelled so good and all the food was just lying there, calling to him.

The hedgehog mother and her hoglets pushed past him and ran up to the nearest cabbage. The mother immediately gobbled up the insects lying around the base of the plants. The hoglets, however, started backing up, lifting their little paws high as they were coated in the fine, sweet smelling dust. First one hoglet, then another, contorted their body and foamed at the mouth. They whipped their head side to side, spraying the foam onto their quills.

Their mother didn't notice. She continued eating, but as she ate, she twitched. Harry saw other hedgehogs drawing near her. He thought they were following the rows of cabbages for the sweet insect feast on the ground, but as they stepped closer and he could see them clearly rather than just blurry shapes, he realised there was something very wrong with the hedgehogs in the field. They moved in a jerky, stiff way, their heads held up and their tiny teeth bared. Each hedgehog had anointed their spines in frothy yellow foam and more leaked from their mouths. Worst of all, their shiny black eyes had all turned a cloudy shade of white.

Harry backed up, his fear overriding the desire to eat. He called a warning to the mother hedgehog, but she didn't seem to hear him. He considered running into the field and nudging the hoglets back to the headland, but he didn't want to get the dust on his paws.

There was something very wrong with the hoglets. They twitched and growled and when Harry looked at them again, he saw their eyes had turned a milky white.

The hedgehog mothered stopped her feasting. The other hogs were almost on top of her. She turned and waddled back to her young, ready to herd them onto another row of cabbages. She nuzzled the nearest hoglet and it latched onto her nose, biting down so hard that blood gushed out of the bite. The hedgehog mother squealed and shook off her hoglet, but the other hoglets now swarmed her. For a moment, Harry thought they wanted to suckle, but then he realised that their mother had tried to roll into a ball to protect herself, but her offspring had sprung upon her and ripped at her soft, unprotected belly. He heard the wet sounds of their chewing and crunching on her flesh.

The other hedgehogs emerged from the rows of cabbages and gathered around the mother and her hoglets. Harry thought they were going to chase the hoglets away and save the mother, even though he knew in his bones it was too late.

They didn't.

They pushed the hoglets aside and buried their noses in the bloody entrails of the mother, ripping and tearing and fighting over her innards while they chuckled and squealed in delight.

Harry froze. He wanted to roll into a ball and be safe, but he knew that wouldn't protect him. He tried to turn and flee, but his legs weren't listening to him. The delicious smell of the field was tainted by the sickening odour of death.

A dozen hedgehogs, two, three surged out of the rows of cabbages, all with cloudy white eyes, snarling mouths and foam-covered spines. The mother and her hoglets were swamped by the hogs trying to get to the feast, but more turned towards the headland, their noses twitching as they searched for new prey.

They turned toward Harry.

Harry found he could move again. He didn't want to be torn to pieces and devoured like a slug. He turned around and ran back to the hedge, the hogs scurrying after him.

CHAPTER 2

The young rabbits had formed into couples and were nuzzling each other as Harry ran towards them shouting.

"Run!"

A large brown buck hopped away from his companion and puffed his chest out at Harry.

"Hey, get lost hog."

"The hedgehogs are coming, get into your burrow."

The other rabbits threw themselves about on the grass laughing.

"What are they going to do, stick us to death with their spines?"

The skinny buck tried to roll into a ball and crashed into the grey doe next to him.

"Oh no, the fearsome hedgehogs are going to eat all our fleas."

A petite doe with incredibly large eyes boxed the air with her front paws and the other rabbits peeled with laughter.

Harry thought he'd hide in their burrow if they weren't going to. He kept running forward while the rabbits made fun. He didn't know where the warren led underground, and he'd normally never enter a rabbit's home, but he knew that they always had a back door and hopefully it would take him far away from the field.

"Hey, Charlie, the hedgehogs are coming."

Harry climbed into the opening of the burrow and turned around to look back over the lip of the hole. The rabbits had stopped messing and hopped into a line looking out over the field. Although their round furry rumps obscured Harry's view, he could still see a wave of blurry shapes surging towards the rabbits, and he could hear their snarls and growls as they stumbled forward.

"There's something wrong with those hedgehogs."

The skinny buck fidgeted, and his back paws drummed on the ground.

"They don't look right. What's wrong with their eyes? And why is there foam all over their quills?"

The grey furred doe backed up towards the burrow. Harry had a vision of her trampling him as she ran into the warren for safety and he reconsidered his decision to hide in the hole. He started climbing out before the six rabbits crushed him as they ran for home.

The doe with the abnormally large eyes raised her head and screamed.

"I smell blood."

Harry felt the rabbits' fear and he knew they were going to bolt, but the big brown buck stood fast.

"Don't be silly, they're only hedgehogs."

The wave of hedgehogs hit him first. They surged into him and latched onto the fur on his chest, nipped at his paws and tried to climb onto his back to bite his delicate ears. He reared up and shook some off, but there were so many pressing against him, they knocked him over onto his side. He kicked out with his back legs, sending several hedgehogs back into the hogs behind them, but another ten replaced each one he knocked back. They dug with their paws at his flesh, searching for the juicy mouthfuls of his intestines. Harry heard the crunch of the rabbit's ears as hedgehogs ripped and tore at the delicate skin. The large buck squealed in pain.

"Charlie."

One of the does jumped towards the buck even as the hedgehogs swarmed him completely and he disappeared beneath a covering of twitching, cloudy eyed creatures. She head butted the nearest hogs and jumped and danced, hitting out with both her front and hind paws. For a moment Harry thought she would be victorious, but there were so many hogs. They seemed to cover the ground in a spiny grass, and no matter how hard they'd been kicked, they got right back up again and kept coming.

The doe panted with the effort of fighting, but the hogs were relentless. Little mouths latched onto her paws and flanks each time she landed and soon the weight of the hogs was too much for her. She couldn't jump again, and her squeals joined the bucks as the hogs bore her to the ground and tore ragged mouthfuls out of her body.

Blood stained the ground and tinged the air with the warning scent of danger.

Harry backed away from the carnage. The other rabbits seemed to have lost their sense. The skinny buck was spinning in circles and the large eyed doe was keening as if she'd already been attacked. The hedgehogs kept coming and swarmed over the rabbits. The last buck and doe turned and bolted for their hole, a look of terror in their eyes.

Harry couldn't watch. He turned and ran. He struggled through the hedge and tumbled down into the ditch on the other side. He still heard the wet sloppy sounds of the rabbits being rendered in the field behind him, and the snarls of the hedgehogs as they followed his scent.

Terror made him pant as he struggled up the steep side of the ditch. He wasn't made for running. He was supposed to roll into a ball and let his spines protect him, but he'd seen that they wouldn't protect him from this danger. He never thought he'd be more afraid of his own kind than a dog or a badger.

He pushed through the long grass at the edge of the ditch. The smell of the field still blocked his senses, even though the new scent of blood and fear made him feel sick to his stomach.

He heard bodies pushing through the hedge behind him, the rustling so loud that he knew the numbers were higher than he could count. The snarling rose all around him. He expected to feel sharp incisors grab his back paws at any moment.

He burst from the long grass and scurried across the short grass verge, moving parallel to the road as he ran away from the field. He thought about making for the river, but hedgehogs were strong swimmers. They would be bound to follow him across.

Rabid hogs crashed through the long grass after him. He raced along the verge, but he was tiring. He couldn't keep running for much longer. He considered rolling into a ball at the bottom of the ditch and hoping they'd pass him by, but he knew they wouldn't. They'd find him and eat him like they had the hedgehog mother and the rabbits.

He heard their squeals of pain, smelled their blood, shuddered at the thought of sharp teeth nipping his flesh and tearing into him, swallowing down his sinew and bone.

He felt sick. He felt sore. He pushed himself forward.

The roar of an approaching engine gave him hope. He knew that those monsters brought death. Little more than a hoglet he'd seen an older male hedgehog try to roll into a ball in protection against such a beast as he crossed the road. The monster ploughed through him, flattened out the old male and left him with his insides on the outsides as it rumbled on. It didn't even stop to eat him or carry off his body for eating later. The experience had chilled Harry to the bone, and he'd avoided the road for days, but it had taught him an important lesson. If the monster comes for you, fight your instinct to protect yourself and keep running.

In many ways the monster was like the hedgehogs that chased him now, and Harry wondered if the monster had infected the hogs in some way. However, he hoped that so many hogs in one place would spur the monster into a frenzy and it would flatten them all, the way the hedgehogs were gorging on the feast lying out for them in the field.

He veered away from the verge and scurried across the hard road even as the eyes of the monster lit up the night and played across his back. He could smell its foul breath heavy on the air. He made it to the other side of the road before it saw him and climbed back onto the grass, moving towards the shadow of the dry-stone wall before he paused and looked back.

The wave of hedgehogs flowed across the verge and ran out onto the road, following his scent. As they turned the road into a seething river of hedgehogs, the monster roared towards them. None froze or rolled into a ball or tried to protect themselves in anyway. They kept coming as if they didn't even hear the monster.

The monster kept coming too. Did Harry hear it roar louder as it sighted its prey? The lights lit up the mass of twitching, foaming, snarling, white eyed hedgehogs, their noses raised as they searched for Harry. Watching from the shadow of the dry-stone wall, Harry shuddered. Then the monster descended on the hedgehogs, crushing them and scattering others. Harry wanted to block his ears to the sound of the hedgehogs splattering onto the blacktop, their bones popping, but before it had begun, it was over. The monster killed indiscriminately and roared away, leaving its foul breath heavy on the air and the sudden darkness from the absence of its eyes.

All Harry could smell was death and the breath of the monster, and the delicious smell of the field that still called to him. He still heard snarling, but he couldn't see anything. The monster's bright eyes had blinded him. He blinked, his eyes tearing up, and slowly his eyes adjusted to the moonlight.

The road was a scene of carnage. Flattened hedgehogs covered the wide surface, their entrails hanging out, their blood painting the hard ground.

Harry felt joy surge through him. He had done it. He had defeated the hedgehogs.

There were still more coming that hadn't been on the road when the monster attacked, but they seemed disorientated by the smell of blood and death and licked at the road surface and nibbled at the bodies of the fallen.

Harry caught his breath. He would sneak away while the remaining hogs were distracted by the dead.

As he moved slowly through the grass in the shadow of the wall, creeping away, afraid to draw the attention of the hogs, he noticed the flattened creatures on the road were twitching. His stomach turned. They mustn't have all been killed outright. Even though they'd been chasing him to tear him to pieces and eat him, he felt sorry for them dying such a slow and painful death.

The hogs didn't seem to be in pain though. They pushed their bodies up with obviously broken legs. Hogs with flattened bodies crawled forward on their bellies. Others pulled loops of intestines after them. How were they still moving? Why where they still coming? What were these things?

Harry watched in wide eyed disbelief as the hogs, seemingly dead and defeated only moments before, lifted their noses and sniffed the air. Growling low, they lurched their battered and broken bodies towards him.

They'd caught his scent and were coming to get him.

CHAPTER 3

H arry hurried to the end of the dry-stone wall and dived into the driveway. The gravel crunched under his paws as he ran for the flowerbeds. He climbed over the wooden edging and wove through the plants, slipping between the garage and the fence to make his way to the back garden. As he ran out from behind the garage, he almost crashed into a dark shape crouched by the shed.

"Watch it."

He blinked and sniffed. He recognised Cassie, the tortoiseshell cat who lived in the house attached to the garden. He'd met her a few times, but mostly he knew her scent from foraging in her garden. He often found a dish of yummy food by the backdoor.

"Cassie, you have to get out of here. The hedgehogs are coming."

The cat blinked her amber eyes. She had very unusual colouring with patches of gold, orange and black on her brown coat. It made her almost invisible in the undergrowth and dappled shadow near the shed.

"What are you talking about, hog?"

Harry paused to catch his breath. The muscles in his legs ached from so much running and he was afraid his heart was going to beat out of his chest with stress. If only he could curl up in his cosy nest and pretend it was all a dream, but the smell of blood was too strong in his nose and he still heard the snarls of the deranged hedgehogs ringing in his ears.

"There's something wrong with the hedgehogs. They're after me and they'll eat you if they catch you."

Cassie growled in the back of her throat. "As I'm not a slug, I think I will be all right. Go find a kitten to frighten with your naptime tales."

The cat struggled with something between her paws and a little face appeared between her toes. Harry jumped as a tiny golden field mouse wriggled her way out of the cat's grip and tried to run away. Before she'd got two mouse lengths, Cassie stretched out her paw and caught her tail, holding her down. Then she jumped in the air, pouncing on the mouse, before rolling on her back and tossing the mouse into the air. She juggled the field mouse from paw to paw before rolling back onto her front and holding the mouse captive under her chest.

"Help me."

The mouse's voice was muffled, but her plaintive call was clear to Harry's ears.

"What have you got there?"

Cassie looked away and blinked a few times.

"None of your business."

Harry snuffled over to the cat and sniffed her paws.

"You've a mouse and you're playing with her. How cruel. Kill her or let her go, but don't torture her."

He heard the mouse squeak in fright at the mention of killing her.

"I'd rather you'd let me go."

Cassie hissed and flattened her body over the mouse, boxing her paws into a prison with the rodent inside.

"Stay out of this, hog."

Harry looked at the cat. She obviously had never gone hungry a day in her life. The fact that she could afford to leave dishes of food untouched outside her house showed that she didn't need to kill the mouse for sustenance. Harry had been raised to abide by the rule that you only ate enough to sustain you. To gorge yourself on more food than necessary was to give into gluttony and playing with your food was wasteful.

"A responsible predator doesn't play with her food. Let the mouse go, there are other hungry animals out tonight who might be in greater need of her than you."

Cassie growled but she sat up and opened her paws. The mouse stayed squatting in front of her, frozen in fright. Cassie opened her mouth and put it around the back of the mouse's neck. The mouse squeaked again and covered her eyes with her paws, but Cassie didn't bite down. She raised her head and shook it.

"I can't."

"You're growing soft, Cassandra."

Roy seemed to materialise out of the shadows that surrounded the shed. He sat down near Harry and curled his bushy tail around his paws.

"It's not that I don't want to, I don't know how to. It is so frustrating. Catching them is easy, but I don't know what to do with them afterwards."

The mouse looked from the cat to the fox in sheer terror. Harry felt sorry for her. He snuffled over and sniffed her.

"I'm Harry. What's your name?"

Her whiskers twitched as she sniffed Harry. She leaned towards him and whispered her name.

"Tina."

Roy looked at the mouse and licked his lips. Harry moved in front of her, feeling protective of Tina. The slaughter of the mother hedgehog and the rabbits made him reluctant to witness anymore killing. He'd had all he could take for one night.

The fox turned his attention to the hedgehog.

"Hey Harry, I'm glad you decided to steer clear of the field. The smell totally freaked me out. I think I'll stay at my winter den for a few days."

Cassie lifted one of her little round paws, which looked so soft now that her claws were hidden beneath her fur, and licked it, before running the paw across her ear and down her face.

"Haven't you heard, Roy, the hedgehogs are coming, and we are all in terrible danger."

Roy's ears swivelled towards Harry.

"What's this? Some kind of hedgehog revolt?"

Cassie continued to wash her face.

"I always thought the hogs were revolting."

Harry felt the muscles under his quills tighten.

"It's the field. It has done something to the hedgehogs. They're attacking everything, even their own. They killed the young rabbits in the hedge burrow, and they chased me across the road. The monster with the shiny eyes flattened some of them, but they just peeled themselves off the road and kept chasing me. It's like they don't feel pain anymore. They'll be here any minute. You should all run."

Roy stared at Harry for a breath and then rolled onto his side. He kicked his legs into the air and wriggled on his back, barking with laughter. Even Cassie purred derisively.

"Oh no, dead hedgehogs are going to get us. Zedhogs, you could call them. Or zogs. They'll gnaw me to death. I'm so frightened."

Tina whispered to Harry.

"I believe you."

Harry wasn't sure if the mouse really believed him or if she was trying to stay close to him until the two larger predators had left. He couldn't blame her. He didn't think he'd be so brave if he sat between a dog and a badger.

"Thank you, Tina. You were right about the field, Roy. There's something wrong with it, and now it has infected the hedgehogs."

Roy pulled back his lips, baring his dagger like teeth.

"I think I'll be all right. These have looked after me so far."

Harry couldn't deny that Roy's teeth were impressive, and he wouldn't want to take them on himself, but the monster had attacked the hedgehogs and hadn't been able to stop them. Foxes couldn't best the monster, not even badgers survived a fight with it.

"They'll be here soon, so I'm going to wish you luck and take my leave."

The fox and cat continued to laugh as Harry hurried away, but Tina stayed with him, scurrying as close to his quills as she could without hurting herself. He expected she'd dash into the undergrowth as soon as they were out of range of Cassie and Roy.

"You should run too."

Tina's whiskers twitched. "I will, and I'll tell my family to warn their friends."

She was a sensible mouse, and Harry was impressed with her. Perhaps they could have been friends under different circumstances.

He left the shadows that cloaked the square between the shed and back of the garage and entered a patch of moonlight that turned the lawn into silver. He smelled the comforting odour of the compost heap. Next to that a leylandii hedge led into the next garden, and Harry would be closer to home.

Behind him, the fence separating the from garden from the back rattled and he heard strange thumps on the paved area by the backdoor. Tina stopped following him and he heard her gasp. He turned around and peered into the darkness near the house. He couldn't see a thing.

"What is it?"

"Hedgehogs. Climbing to the top of the fence and then flinging themselves down the other side. They must be hurting themselves, but they don't seem to care. What's wrong with them, Harry?"

It was so unlike hedgehogs to jump from heights. While a strong climber, Harry found it much harder to go down than up, as did all his kind.

Tina trembled and clasped her paws around her muzzle.

"There are so many of them. It's like it's raining hedgehogs."

Harry nudged the little field mouse.

"Get out of here, Tina, before it's too late."

She squeaked and even Harry squealed in fright as two large bodies crashed out of the shadows next to them and ran onto the grass. Roy and Cassie. Both the cat and the fox had the hair along their back standing on end, making them appear bigger, and Harry smelled blood on them, although he didn't know if it belonged to them or the hogs.

Roy snarled, his teeth bared, and his eyes focused with a killer's gaze.

"They're here."

They weren't laughing at Harry anymore. As they stood together, a wave of hedgehogs stumbled out from behind the garage and flowed toward them. Some looked intact, apart from their strange eyes and foam flecked backs, but many others dragged broken limbs and soft body parts that weren't supposed to see the light of the moon.

Cassie hissed and danced on her tiptoes, her hair fluffed out and her tail ramrod straight in the air as if she'd been struck by lightning.

"To the house, quick."

CHAPTER 4

C assie raced across the grass, leapt onto the patio, and disappeared into the house. Roy bounded after her. Harry knew he couldn't keep running from the hedgehogs, and even though the house seemed a scary place to hide, he suspected it would be safe. He hurried after the cat and the fox and was surprised that Tina came with him.

Tina spoke as they ran for the house.

"I have family who live there."

The hedgehogs snarled and slobbered, foam dripping from their mouths, drawing closer on both sides. Harry and Tina arrived at the house, but it looked impenetrable. Where had Cassie and Roy disappeared to and how did they get inside?

Tina darted to a tiny hole near the outside tap.

"In here."

Harry shook his head. Even with his spines pressed flat, he would never be able to squeeze into such a hole.

"I can't fit."

He turned around, facing the hogs that crawled nearer, gnashing their teeth, and snarling, their heads waving in the air as they followed the scent of their prey. He thought he would roll into a ball after all. He didn't want to go down without a fight.

"Go, Tina, save yourself."

The mouse hesitated. She turned away from the tiny opening and crouched behind him, rubbing her paws together.

"I don't want to leave you, Harry."

It was foolish for her to endanger herself for him, but Harry was touched. He was about to nudge her into the opening with his nose when Roy's head appeared in what Harry assumed was the wall of the house.

"What's keeping you? Quick, in through the cat door."

Tina turned and jumped through the cat door in a flash, but Harry took his time climbing up the step and through the high ledge of the little opening cut in the larger door. He tried to move as quickly as he could, but he'd never used a cat door before it and he found it difficult to navigate.

Roy kept the door open with his head, peering over Harry to the approaching hogs.

"Faster, Harry. Faster would be better."

He was too slow. The livelier hedgehogs, who hadn't been flattened by the monster, surged through the cat door just as Harry tumbled inside the house. They didn't seem to mind the step and the high lip of the cat door. Perhaps it wasn't that they navigated it better than Harry, but they threw themselves through the opening without thought of pain or injury.

Cassie stood on the other side of the door hissing and swiping at Roy to back away from the opening.

"Quick, get it closed."

Harry looked around. He stood in an alcove with wellies and shoes in a row on one side and coats hanging on hooks above his head, while an enormous space stretched away from him on the other side. Cassie's scent was everywhere, as well as human, and dog.

Dog! Cassie lived with a dog? He almost turned around and threw himself on the mercy of the rabid hedgehogs.

Roy crouched back on his haunches and the cat door slapped closed, but the hogs kept piling up on the other side and spilling into the house. The first ones through bit Roy's paws, and the fox howled in pain.

Tina hid among the shoes. She beckoned to Harry with her paws.

"Over here."

Harry hurried over to her, slipping on the tiled floor that felt cold under his paws. He didn't think the shoes looked like a very good hiding place, but when he got to Tina, he saw another mouse hole in the baseboard behind the footwear.

"My cousin Artie lives here. He'll find somewhere safe for us to hide."

Tina looked hopeful, but Harry shook his head.

"I can't fit into that hole either. You should go though. If it's too small for me, the other hedgehogs won't fit either. Not even the flat ones."

The field mouse looked between Harry and the opening, as if she couldn't believe any animal would be too big to fit through such a palatial opening.

"There must be somewhere else we will be safe."

Harry looked back at the door. Roy, in his efforts to snap at the hedgehogs and leap out of the way of their jaws, had knocked over the wellies and trapped some of the hogs underneath. Cassie pushed her front paws against the cat door, trying to hold back the press of hedgehogs on the other side.

A strong smell, one that terrified Harry and loosened his bowels, announced the arrival of a dog. She rushed out of the shadows, her white teeth flashing as she barked at Roy and tried to nip his hindlegs.

"Fox! Out, out, foul fiend! How dare you enter my domain?"

A couple of hedgehogs waddled towards the spaniel and latched onto her front paws. She whined, then lowered her head and latched onto the nearest hog. She grasped it by the head, picked it up and flung it across the room, where it hit the coats and tumbled to the floor. She shook her paw, trying to dislodge the second hog, before grabbing it by its leg and tossing it towards the far corner where Harry and Tina trembled in fear.

Harry couldn't help it. He had to roll into a ball. Could this night get any worse?

"A dog. Cassie never said she lived with a dog."

Cassie struggled to keep the cat door closed, but she fought a losing battle.

"Help me keep them out, Merry."

The dog snarled, her attention back on Roy. Her hackles rose along her back.

"I'll rout this fiend. I'll send his red hide back to where it belongs, and he will rue the day he decided to set paw inside the den of Merry."

Cassie sighed.

"Dogs. The fox is a friend. Help me against the hedgehogs, you dog brain."

Merry looked at the fox, and then looked at the hedgehogs she had savaged. Already they were getting to their feet. The first hog, which had landed in the coats, attacked the closest living creature. Roy shrieked in pain as the hog latched onto his back leg with a strong bite. He tried to shake the hog loose. The second hog crawled towards Harry and Tina where they huddled by the mouse hole.

Finally understanding the hedgehogs were attacking, the spaniel ran to Cassie and pawed at something metal along the base of the cat door.

"Engage the bolt."

Cassie looked down at the metal and hissed in exasperation as Merry's paws kept on missing the bolt.

"Hold the door."

The cat and the dog swapped places. Merry forced her body against the cat door, holding it closed against the growing stream of hedgehogs on the other side. With the extra weight of the spaniel holding the door flush with its frame, Cassie's nimble paws had no difficulty in driving the bolt home. Once locked, Merry backed away from the cat door. All the animals watched the little door to see if it would hold. The flexible material bowed under the pressure of the hedgehogs leaning against it, but it held.

Merry sniffed at the cat door.

"We should push something against it to be extra safe."

Cassie ran to the other end of the alcove. Harry noticed a large bag set against the wall. The cat leaned her body into the heavy bag and tried to push it over to the door.

"Help me."

Merry danced on the spot, clearly agitated.

"Not my dogfood."

Roy whined as he gripped the hog attached to his back leg, the creature's spines pricking his muzzle, and he ripped it away from his flesh in a shower of blood. The hog rolled into the remaining wellies, trapping itself under the boot. As the fox whirled around, looking for any other hogs, his long tail knocked the heavy coats off their hooks and they fell onto the hog beside Harry just as it was about to attack, imprisoning it in folds of waxed cloth.

Cassie succeeded in moving the bag of dogfood a tiny bit, but it would take her months to reach the door at that rate.

"Help me, Roy."

Roy gripped the top of the bag in his teeth and it toppled onto its side. While he pulled and Cassie pushed, they manoeuvred it in front of the cat door.

Cassie sat back, panting.

"There, that ought to hold them."

Merry growled, but she turned away and trotted into the wide space beyond the alcove, her nails clicking on the tiles. Harry heard her lapping water at a distance, and he realised he was thirsty and hungry too.

Cassie and Roy followed the dog into the next room. Harry looked at Tina.

"You should go to your cousin. You'll be safer with your own kind."

Tina washed her face, drawing her paws down her muzzle and through her long whiskers. "I won't leave until I know you are safe, Harry."

Harry felt pessimistic about the odds of that happening soon.

"You might be here for a long time."

Tina twitched her nose.

"That's all right. There's plenty of nice food in here."

Judging by the smell, none of it would be food that Harry could eat. Maybe Cassie knew where he could find more of the nice food that he found outside the house most nights.

It was hot inside the house, but Harry felt a breeze blowing around the large space from somewhere high above his head. The tiles were slippery, and his feet kept on sliding out from underneath him, and he'd land on his belly on the cold floor. Forests of wooden pillars stretched up into the sky in the middle of the room, but the trees were dead and leafless, their roots squared off and sitting on the sterile tile.

Harry kept to the edge of the room, slowly making his way along the wall. Roy jumped onto the broad canopy that topped the forest of wooden poles and licked his wounds. Merry sat on something soft and nest like and licked her paws, stopping to look up at Roy and growl. Harry turned around when he smelled Merry close by and scurried back the way he had come.

At the other end of the room the walls grew closer together and Harry could smell mice behind the wooden walls. Cassie jumped up a series of steep steps and stood on a cliff edge above him, gazing out a window. The breeze was stronger here, and Harry liked it, but it brought with it the scent of death and hedgehogs.

Cassie popped her head out the window and looked out at the garden.

"They're surrounding the house. There are so many of them. Where did they all come from?"

Harry heard Roy moving from his perch, but the fox was a blurry shape in the distance, lit by the moonlight falling through the far window.

"They're swarming around down here too."

Tina gripped Harry's spines with her front paws.

"They'll be gone by morning, won't they? Hedgehogs sleep during the day, don't they?"

Harry hoped that would be the case. Normally all healthy hogs would be cuddled up in their nest before dawn, but there was nothing normal or healthy about the things outside. What had Roy called them? Zogs? He didn't want to upset Tina.

"I hope so."

Harry wanted to see what was happening outside for himself. He started climbing up the ledges he had watched Cassie jump on to get to the high cliff. Tina easily ran up the side of the counter and waited for him at the top.

Somewhere on the other side of the room, Merry cleared her throat with an ugly hacking cough.

"What has happened to the hedgehogs? My paws really hurt from their bites. I'm going to be mad if I have to go to the V E T because of this."

Cassie moved away from the window and peered into the shadowy room.

"There's something in the field that turned them into these things."

Roy sneezed. Harry heard the fox's nails tapping on the wooden surface where he stood looking out the far window.

"Something bad is in that field. I can smell it on the hogs and now it's on me. I can feel it in my blood like a sickness."

Merry whined.

"I bet those hedgehogs haven't had their shots, Cassie. What if I get sick because they bit me?"

Cassie flicked her tail side to side, knocking into the bottles and pots lined up along the windowsill.

"You'll be fine, Merry. You aren't a hedgehog."

Harry heard the dog's claws click across the tiles and he was glad he had almost reached Cassie when Merry's blurry form swam into view below him.

"What if it isn't only hedgehogs who get sick?"

Cassie's tail swished more aggressively.

"Don't worry, that won't happen."

Harry gained the countertop. It was cluttered with lots of different dishes and metal instruments and glass containers. Tina moved through them with ease, but Harry found it more difficult to navigate. His paws hit metal and he peered down into a huge pit with smooth, polished metal sides and a mound of dishes at the bottom. Grateful he hadn't fallen in, he skirted the edge towards Cassie and the window. A loud thump behind him and Merry's head appearing over the edge of the counter, her breath hot on his back, made him stumble and he slipped, catching himself on a hard lump near the window. Immediately a loud waterfall gushed out of a strange, curved metal stalk beside him.

Cassie moved to let Harry and Tina join her at the window. The moans of the hedgehogs outside set Harry's teeth on edge. He looked out at the foaming, twitching, snarling mass of hedgehogs. He didn't even know there were that many hogs in the area. The enticing smell of the field must have drawn them from miles around.

Tina crept out the window and sat on the windowsill outside. She squeaked and hurried back to Harry.

"They're climbing the wall. They're going to get inside."

Harry pushed his head out the window and looked down. It was true. Many of the hogs had climbed up the wooden sides of a flowerbed beside the window and were now crawling up a tree that grew against the wall of the house to gain access to their prey inside.

As Harry tried to scuttle backwards, he knocked over a bottle that rolled out the window and fell onto the nearest hogs, knocking them back.

Cassie meowed in delight. Harry felt her breath on his back, and she leaned out the window above him.

"Great idea, hog. Throw more things at them."

CHAPTER 5

Harry scuttled back inside, knocking over the pots, and spilling weird sticks and spongy stones onto the windowsill. Cassie hooked them with her claws and flung them out the window. She yowled every time her throw was successful, and she hit her target.

"I need more, Harry."

He looked down the windowsill. A group of bottles stood at the far end, as well as a strange looking brush. Tina ran with him and helped knock over the bottles and roll them back to Cassie. The cat caterwauled triumphantly as she sent the bottles flying out the window with swift swings of her paw.

Once the windowsill was empty, Harry turned to the dishes cluttering the countertop. He was too small to lift them, he didn't think he could push them very far. Maybe towards the edge of the cliff inside the house, but not up to the window beside Cassie. He was thrilled when Roy jumped onto the counter beside him. The fox was large enough and strong enough to pick up the dishes and fling them out at the hogs trying to climb in the window.

Cassie turned away from the hogs and looked back into the house.

"I need more, Harry. They're climbing back up."

Harry turned to the fox to ask for his help and outline his plan, but he realised there was something very wrong with Roy. He twitched, his whole body spasming from his head to his tail. Foam flecked his lips, and his dark eyes had turned a solid, milky white.

Roy turned to Cassie, grabbed her in his jaws and picked her up. Harry stumbled backwards. He felt Tina trembling beside him. Cassie struggled in Roy's grip. Harry had never seen a cat twist and wriggle with such manic fury. She screeched and raked her claws across Roy's face and chest, but the fox no longer seemed to notice pain. Her movements dislodged her from his mouth with a great rending of flesh and a spurt of blood. Her momentum carried her over the edge of the counter, and she disappeared into the room.

Roy gobbled up the lump of meat torn from Cassie's neck, sniffed the air and turned towards Harry and Tina.

Harry stumbled backwards, away from the fox.

"Run, Tina."

His feet scrabbled for purchase against the countertop, but it was too slippery, and he slipped back over the edge. He clung on for one agonising moment. He looked into Tina's face and the little mouse placed her paws over his, and then he fell down into the shadows.

Luckily, the ledges he'd used to climb up caught him and he bumped and rolled painfully to the floor. Tina scurried behind him, evading Roy's jaws by a whisker length as they snapped closed where she had sat moments before.

Cassie lay twitching and frothing at the mouth on the floor, Merry standing over her. The spaniel's eyes had also clouded over, her mouth hung open and foaming drool gathered around her lip folds.

Tina pressed her face close to Harry's and sniffed his nose.

"Harry, are you all right?"

Harry struggled to his feet. Everything hurt. Roy loomed above, and Merry blocked his way ahead. He knew at any moment Cassie would rise and join the other two animals.

"Yes, but I don't think I will be for much longer."

Tina turned around and dashed into the corner. A large metal box that smelled of food hummed among the wooden walls. Harry followed her, but he was forced to move slowly because of the slippery tiles that kept stealing his paws from under him.

"There's another hole here. They won't be able to follow."

The mouse disappeared into a gap between the metal box and the baseboard. She turned around and sat up, rubbing her paws together.

"Come on, Harry. You must be able to fit in here. There's more room behind this thing so you don't have to worry once you get through this narrow passage, it opens up a lot."

Harry knew he wouldn't be able to fit into such a small space. His spines would stick out and get caught on the sides of the passageway, no matter how hard he tried to keep them flat along his back. However, the three snarling beasts behind him was enough incentive to make him try. He didn't want to be torn apart, and he knew that a dog, a fox, and a cat would make short work of him if he tried.

He ran toward the hole as fast as he dared. At the last step he slipped and he slid across the tile headfirst into the hole. His whiskers brushed against the sides of the opening, but his nose fit in, then his head up to his ears barrelled towards Tina. The mouse backed up, and Harry saw the happiness in her body language mirror his own hope.

He pressed his quills tight to his back and stretched out his front paws, feeling the sides of the tunnel scrape painfully against his back and shoulders. Once he had slid in up to his withers, he could go no further, he was stuck. He tried to push with his hindlegs, but he was just too big. It hurt if he tried to force his body any further into the hole, and he was now stuck, prone and vulnerable, with his rump and hindlegs sticking out into the room.

He felt Roy land on the tiles and heard the predators sniffing as they searched the room for him.

Tina ran up and pressed her paws to his.

"Come on, Harry. It's only a little further."

Harry felt so scared, he didn't know if he could speak. He didn't want Tina to know how frightened he was. He tried to sound calm, but instead he sounded squeaky and strange.

"I can't. I'm stuck, but I think I've fit enough of my body into the tunnel that I'll be okay."

Tina sat up and ran her paws along the rough walls of the passageway.

"Maybe Artie could ask his friends to make the tunnel wider. If we all chewed together, and there were enough of us..."

Harry sighed and rested his chin on the rough floor of the passage.

"No, Tina. There isn't time, and it would be wrong to put your friends at risk. Go to your cousin. Warn the other animals about the hedgehogs. Tell them what happens when you get bitten."

Tina washed her face, rubbing at her eyes with closed paws.

"I don't want to leave you, Harry. You saved me from the cat. I owe you my life."

Harry closed his eyes. He really wanted to roll into a ball, but he was trapped stretched out on his belly with his head in a hole and his rump sticking out for all to see. He wondered if being torn apart would hurt much.

"Then run away and live. Spread the word. Save as many animals as you can."

Tina squeaked in distress, but she backed away from Harry. As she faded into a blur, he could just make her out as she turned and disappeared up the passageway with a flick of her long tail.

So this was it. Harry resigned himself to his fate. He felt the floor vibrate and realised Roy had found him. He was glad in a way. The fox had the biggest jaws and should make the quickest meal of him. He hoped that they would tear him up and eat him because he didn't want to become one of those things, especially not like the flattened hogs with their insides on the outside.

Teeth latched on to Harry's hindleg. He wanted to be brave, but it hurt so much he screamed. Strong jaws tried to drag him from the tunnel. Some of his quills broke or were pulled out, caught on the rough walls of the passage, as the fox yanked him from the hole. He got stuck a couple of times as Roy tried to extract him, his spines, like hooks, digging into the walls as he moved backwards. Harry was sure his leg would be pulled off before he made it out of the hole, but with one last tug the fox freed him from the mouse hole.

The sudden release of the hedgehog caused the fox's head to snap up, and Harry felt himself flying up into the air. He looked down and saw three sets of jaws open and waiting for him, but his trajectory carried him over the hungry mouths and towards the window. For a moment, Harry was afraid he'd crash out the window and land, mangled and bleeding, on the flowerbed full of raging hogs. He didn't fly that far, however. Instead, he fell into the metal pit, which was now full to the brim with water.

CHAPTER 6

H arry fell into the water with a splash. Everything hurt as he dunked down below the surface, and then he bobbed back up and he could breathe.

The waterfall poured from the metal stalk and filled up the pit, but the volume of water was too great to be contained by the pit and water gushed over the sides, dribbling down the cliff to the floor.

Harry tread water, afraid to leave the pool. First Roy's questing nose, then Merry's and finally Cassie's appeared at the edge of the counter. Their cloudy eyes sightless, their twitching noses searched for the prey they knew was close but which they couldn't locate. He thought it was something to do with the water that masked his scent, but his leg hurt with each kick and he knew he had been bitten so it was only a matter of time before he turned into one of those things. His safety was temporary.

The overflowing water carried him close to the edge of the pool, and every time Roy or Merry or Cassie appeared, sniffing for him, he'd splash backwards in fright, sending water cascading over the animals until the fur on their faces was wet through.

He wondered how long it would take for him to turn. What would they do once they were all milky eyed monsters? Would they dig through the walls to get to Tina and her cousin? Maybe they'd climb out the window to join the hogs and roam across the countryside tearing apart the animals they stumbled upon, making more of their kind if any animal was unlucky enough to be bitten and lucky enough to get away.

After a while he noticed that the faces of Cassie, Merry and Roy were no longer appearing at the edge of the counter. Had they stopped looking for him?

The water sapped his energy, leeching his warmth from him, and his leg ached from being pulled out of the mouse hole. He needed to get out of the pool. He waited to see if he had been imagining things, but his attackers remained still and silent out of sight of the pool.

Harry let the rushing water carry him to the edge of the pool and braced his legs against the slippery metal walls. He looked out, but he couldn't see anything moving in the shadows below him.

He swam to the side of the pool and climbed out onto the dishes, sprawling across them. After resting for a little while and catching his breath, he crept across the countertop and peered down at the floor. The water gushed over the cliff edge and pooled on the tiles below. He saw dark shapes lying in the water, but he couldn't make them out. They didn't seem to be moving.

Had the creatures, unable to locate him in the water, given up and gone to sleep? Was it possible?

Harry crept closer to the edge, but his sore leg snagged on one of the dishes cluttering the countertop. It slid towards him. He tried to jump out of the way, but they both fell off the cliff. The dish crashed to the tiles with a loud bang, but once again Harry managed to arrest his fall by bumping down the climbing ledges he'd used to follow Cassie up to the window.

The water lay in a shallow puddle across the bottom of the cliff. On the far side of the cracked dish, Harry could make out the still forms of Roy, Merry and Cassie. He could smell them too, and for the first time in hours his head felt clear of the stench of the field. Roy, Merry and Cassie smelled as they should too.

The noise of the falling dish seemed to have roused the creatures, however. Roy's head rose, and his eyes shone in the moonlight coming through the window.

Harry wanted to meet death on his own terms. He couldn't escape again, that was certain. He rolled into a ball.

He heard paws splashing through water and a nose gently nudged him.

"Harry, you in there?"

Roy. Roy was talking again, and none of the creatures talked. Harry thought of the eyeshine when Roy had looked at him. The milky, cloudy eyes couldn't reflect light.

Cautiously he unrolled. Roy, soaked to the skin, stood in front of him, his ears all lopsided and his tongue lolling out of his mouth, but definitely Roy and not one of the creatures. Behind him, an equally wet Merry frowned at the water pooling on the tiles, while Cassie had stood up and was slowly making her way across the slippery floor on unsteady paws.

"Roy? Is that really you?"

The fox yipped and spun in a circle, then slipped on the wet tiles and fell over.

"Yup, it's me."

Harry shook his head.

"But how is this possible? What happened?"

Roy sat up, his legs splayed like a new born fawn as he tried to gain purchase on the tiles.

"I've no idea. Maybe it wears off after a while?"

Harry shook the water from his head.

"No, that can't be it. The hedgehogs outside are still white eyed and foaming at the mouth."

Merry licked her lips loudly.

"I believe it is because of the superior canine constitution that was able to repel the disease before it progressed too far."

Somewhere in the far reaches of the room, Cassie hissed.

Harry turned around and bit at his sore leg.

"No, that can't be it either. Roy is a fox and Cassie is a cat, and I was bitten and I'm a hedgehog, but I haven't turned. I don't think I will either, I feel fine, apart from my leg."

Roy hung his head.

"Sorry about that."

Harry grunted. He didn't blame Roy for what had happened when he was sick. In fact, it could have been much worse. He kept replaying his flight through the air, landing in the water, and then Roy, Cassie, and Merry searching for him. What had happened to make them stop jumping up at the counter? What had cured them of the sickness?

"It's the water."

Roy cocked his head onto the side.

"What? How?"

Merry lowered her head and lapped from the puddle she lay in.

"Tastes like ordinary water to me."

Harry wove side to side, excited as he worked out the steps in his head.

"It has to be the water. You kept searching for me, but you couldn't find me, even though I was right in front of your noses. There was something about the water that masked my scent from you, but I think it also washed the infection out of your bodies once you got wet enough. That's why I haven't turned either. I was swimming in the pool for a long time. It must be a poison rather than an illness."

He remembered the powder covering the field and the hoglets getting it all over their paws as they followed their mother to the feast of creepy crawlies.

"It was a poison. The farmer must have put something on the field to kill the slugs and beetles to stop them from eating his cabbages. That's what made it smell so nice."

Roy pulled a face and made a sound like he was getting sick.

"Smelled nice to you, perhaps."

Harry ignored him. His brain was moving so fast, slotting puzzle pieces together, that he could hardly keep up. It must have been the smell of the field that kept him from working it out earlier. Even though he hadn't turned into one of the creatures, just smelling the field must have done something to his head.

"I think the smell attracted the insects so that they'd touch the powder and die, and that's why it drew us hedgehogs to it. It smelled like food, but once we touched the powder or ate the dead bugs we got poisoned, and the poison transferred via the foam into you three when you got bitten."

Cassie appeared at the edge of the pool, lifting her paws carefully to stay clear of the spreading water.

"That may be true, but how did the water rid us of this poison?"

Harry took small steps to either side, afraid to pace too far in case he slipped.

"I think the water washed the poison from us and cleared it from our systems. It's the only thing that makes sense."

Roy yawned, and Harry shuddered as he saw once again how wide the fox's jaws spread and how sharp his teeth were. He had come too close to falling into that mouth.

"I for one am happy that the water washed away the poison, but I'm still trapped in this house and it will be bad for me if I'm still here when the sun comes up and the humans wake."

Harry shook, and his quills clicked faintly as he settled them back into place. His back and sides were badly bruised from being pulled out of the hole, and he knew he would be sore for days to come.

"Don't you see, it is much more important than that. If the water washed the poison off us, it could save the other hedgehogs too. We can save them all."

He didn't know if he could save them all, he wasn't sure if the hogs that had been flattened by the monster would ever be all right again, but he would do his best to save as many as he could.

Cassie purred with laughter.

"How, exactly, are we going to get all the water from the sink to the hedgehogs outside?"

Merry finally stood up and shook herself vigorously, showering the whole room with water.

"It is a great idea, little hedgehog, and I support you. There's a tap outside by the backdoor. Turn that on and it'll soak all the hedgehogs."

Harry nodded.

"Thank you, Merry. That sounds like a plan."

He slid away from the counter and skidded over to the metal box. Droplets of his blood spotted the tiles and walls around the hole. He knew Tina was probably far away by now, but she had said there was a cavity behind the box and maybe she'd gathered with the other mice there. If he could tell her about the cure, she could get the mice to spread it to all the animals.

"Tina."

He pushed his face into the hole, being careful not to go too far in case he got caught again.

"Tina, I don't know if you can hear me. I've found a cure. It's water. Water leeches the toxins from the body and turns you back to a normal animal, not one of the creatures. If you can hear me, Tina, or one of Tina's family, please spread the word. Tell the animals to go to the river and jump in. They'll be safe, and if they've been bitten, they'll be cured."

He heard scurrying at the end of the passageway, but no mouse appeared, and no voice called back to him. After waiting a few more minutes, he turned around and waddled across the room to where Roy, Merry and Cassie waited in the alcove by the backdoor.

"All right, let's do this."

CHAPTER 7

Merry and Roy each grabbed a corner of the bag of dog food and dragged it away from the cat door. Cassie sat by the bolt and raised her paw.

"As soon as I open this, all the hogs are going to rush into the room."

Roy bared his teeth. He crouched by the door, his fur bristled along his back.

"Cassie, you and I should draw as many as we can into the other room and get them into the water. Clear the way for Merry and Harry to get outside and turn on the tap."

Merry stood in front of the cat door, her tail wagging. Harry didn't know if she was excited or afraid. He was a mixture of both. He wasn't looking forward to risking being torn apart by going outside, but the thought of working with a dog filled him with even more fear. If someone had told him when he woke up that night he would be working with a dog before night end, he would never have believed them.

He felt movement by the shoes, and he turned, expecting one of the hogs to have escaped from their wellie prison, but it was Tina. She slipped out of the hole behind the shoes and ran over to him.

"Harry, I'm so glad you're alive. Artie found me and told me what you said. I want to go with you to save the other hedgehogs."

Harry was moved that she'd come back, but she was too little and there were too many hogs out there.

"You should stay here, Tina. It's too dangerous outside. You need to spread the word about the cure."

Tina rubbed her paws across her ears.

"Artie is organising the others to do that. I want to stay with you, Harry, until all the hedgehogs are cured."

She was a brave mouse, Harry had to give her that. He turned back to Cassie.

"Open it, Cassie."

The cat looked at all the animals in front of her, and then opened the bolt with a flick of her paw. The bulging cat door pushed inwards with the weight of all the hedgehogs piled onto the other side and a lumpy mass of spines and snapping jaws, foaming mouths and bloody, broken body parts surged into the house.

Cassie yowled and jumped, batting the hedgehogs with her paws, and luring them into the next room and the spreading water. Roy pounced and snapped, picking up hogs and flinging them into the room over Cassie's head. They fought valiantly, but there were too many hedgehogs. Harry saw Cassie falling over, dragged down by half a dozen hogs latched on to her hindlegs and tail. Roy still spun and bit, but he was bleeding from multiple wounds on his paws and Harry saw hedgehogs hanging from his bushy tail like giant burrs.

Merry barked and forged ahead into the sea of hedgehogs, knocking them from Cassie's back and flinging them towards the water with her wildly snapping jaws. With her help, the tide turned, and a clear path opened to the cat door.

Tina turned to Harry.

"We have to go now, before more hedgehogs clog the door."

Harry felt frozen to the spot. He knew Tina was right, but he didn't know if he could face the creatures outside without the dog by his side.

"We're too small. We won't be able to turn on the tap."

Tina placed her paw against Harry's cheek.

"You can do it, Harry. I believe in you."

Harry tried to stop his legs from shaking.

"We have to try."

Slipping past the hedgehogs that surged after Merry, Cassie and Roy, Harry followed Tina through the cat door. The mouse ran ahead, flowing across the paving to a drain by the side of the house. Harry paused on the step, looking out at the garden. He could smell hedgehogs all around him, and he could see their blurry forms drawing closer. They snarled and moaned, hungry for the animals in the house.

Hungry for him.

He climbed carefully down the step and followed Tina as quickly as he could with his sore leg. Once he reached the drain he looked up at the wall of the house to where the tap stood proud of the building many hedgehog lengths above his head.

"How are we going to reach that?"

Tina grabbed the rough surface of the wall and easily scampered halfway to the tap.

"Come on, Harry. I won't be able to turn the tap by myself."

Harry looked behind him. The hogs were near enough now that he could see their milky eyes and foam flecked backs.

"How am I going to get up there?"

Another flowerbed rested against the wall of the house, its wooden walls rising to tap height. Harry didn't know if he would be able to climb down again, but if he didn't succeed in curing the hedgehogs, he wouldn't want to anyway.

He walked over to the flowerbed and pulled himself onto the narrow ledge of the first plank of wood. It was hard to balance, he wasn't built for such acrobatics, but he kept his footing and managed to climb onto the next plank.

Tina shouted encouragement to him from the tap.

"Come on, Harry. Not much further."

He heard the hogs reach the back door. Most seemed to be moving into the house, but others had caught his scent and followed him to the flowerbed. He knew they wouldn't worry about climbing down from the height, all they cared about was satisfying their craving for flesh. He resisted looking down and climbed the last plank onto the flowerbed.

Tina cheered from her perch on the tap.

"Nearly there."

Harry caught his breath and turned towards the tap. From the ground, the tap looked like an easy stretch from the flowerbed, but now that he had made the climb, the distance yawned like a chasm.

Below him, the foaming jaws of the hogs snapped as they tried to find him and Tina. From the way they had climbed towards the window of the house, Harry knew it wouldn't be long before they scaled the flowerbed and dug into his entrails.

Tina wrapped her tail around the tap and leaned out across the chasm towards Harry.

"Look, it isn't far to reach. Just stretch out you front paws and grip onto the wheel. I can move it a little, so I think with both of us pushing it should turn easily."

Harry looked down at his long feet with his little black claws at the ends of his toes. He didn't have flexible paws like Tina. He didn't know if he could grip the wheel with enough strength to push it as well as support himself.

He had to try.

He waddled to the edge of the flowerbed. He was sure he would fall as soon as he launched his front paws out into the air. He closed his eyes and took a leap of faith. He felt nothing, only empty air under his paws, and then he felt the cold metal of the tap catching his weight and he opened his eyes.

Tina ran her paw over the fine hairs on his face.

"You did it, Harry. Now, push towards the wall. We have to push together."

Harry couldn't breathe. He was afraid that any movement would unbalance him, and he would lose his footing and fall. Tina moved position on the tap so that she faced the wall and her paws rested over his. He felt her push, and he leaned into his front paws. For a moment, nothing happened, and then the wheel of the tap started to move.

"We're doing it."

The mouse's face was set with effort.

"Keep pushing, Harry. Almost there."

Harry concentrated so hard on his forepaws gripping the tap and turning it, he forgot about his sore leg. He shifted his weight to apply more pressure to the tap, he heard water gurgling and a big fat drop appeared on the rim of the tap below him, but then his sore leg gave out and he overbalanced. He grabbed for the tap, Tina grabbed for his paws, but his stubby claws slipped off the cold metal. He fell onto the drain and hit it hard.

He'd failed.

The hogs moaned and surged towards him, circling the drain.

CHAPTER 8

Tina squeaked his name. Harry hoped she'd stay on the tap where she was safe from the hogs. The air had been knocked from his lungs by the fall, but apart from more bruises, he didn't think he was injured. He almost wished he had been killed by the fall, because then he wouldn't have to worry about being torn apart by his own kind.

The hogs sniffed the air, drawn by his scent, and they swarmed the drain. He felt teeth bite down on his hind paw.

He pulled his paw away and curled into a ball, his spines pointed out towards the hogs and his belly pressed into the depression where the drain met the wall of the house.

Teeth gnawed at this quills and paws pulled at his body, trying to get into the soft meat inside him.

The night lit up around Harry momentarily, even through the little gap between his body and the wall he could see the bright flash of light. A moment later, thunder shook the sky. The hogs continued attacking Harry, trying to pull him away from the wall, get past his quills to his flesh.

More lightning followed by another mighty crash of thunder. Something hit the ground beside Harry's head, then the wall above him. The third drop hit him, huge and hard and wet.

Rain.

It had started to rain.

After the first smattering of raindrops, the heavens opened and the water beat against the earth, as if Harry had managed to open the tap in the sky when he'd failed to turn on the one in the garden. The thunderstorm raged above the house and moved on, breaking the oppressive heat, and showering the ground with cooling, healing rain.

Harry kept tucked into his ball, not daring to believe that the rain was real. He started to shiver as the water soaked him, bringing down his temperature. The noises of the hogs, drowned out by the thunder and the heavy rainfall, were now silent for another reason. He couldn't feel the questing paws or the biting jaws anymore.

Slowly, he unrolled and stood up. Water covered the ground and splashed into his face, making his vision even more blurry than usual. It gurgled around his paws, flowing down the drain beneath him.

Bodies of hogs covered the patio. Some looked like they were sleeping, but others looked dead. Flattened, broken, bloodied, their little bodies wouldn't rise again.

Harry saw movement coming towards him and tensed, but it was Tina, running down the wall from the tap and moving to his side.

"You did it, Harry."

He shook the water from his face.

"I didn't do this."

Slowly, the sleeping hogs woke up and shook the rain from their soaked bodies. They looked around, blinking eyes that were once again kind and dark. Bruised, confused, perhaps slightly embarrassed, they turned and filtered out of the garden until only the remains of the fallen hogs still littered the paved area.

Tina pulled at the hairs around Harry's ears.

"Come on, let's go inside."

Harry didn't want to go into the house again, but he had to see if Roy, Cassie and Merry needed any help. Tina scurried across the wet paving and disappeared at the doorstep, while Harry followed her more slowly. It was going to take him a while before he was back to full health.

He climbed up the step and pushed through the cat door. He followed the smell of hedgehogs into the large room. Water sloshed around his paws as he walked. The tiles seemed littered with the bodies of sleeping hogs. He wondered if it took longer for the water in the house to free the hogs from the poison, or if it just took longer for them to get wet enough that the badness would pour out of them.

"Harry."

He looked up. Dark shapes on the top of the strange wooden pillars resolved into Roy and Cassie. The fox pricked his ears forward and called out again.

"Did you do it? Did you turn on the tap?"

Harry lifted his head and shouted up at the fox.

"No, but it started to rain. That did an even better job."

Merry appeared from between the forest of wooden pillars. Harry had to restrain himself from rolling into a ball. He could never get used to being around a dog.

"Time to get these animals out of my house."

Harry agreed. He made the slow, difficult journey through the rising water to greet each hedgehog as they woke up. Some wouldn't wake, either because they'd been flattened by the monster or too badly injured by Roy and Merry. Most of the hedgehogs seemed to be none the worse for being poisoned. They kept their heads down and followed Harry to the cat door and stumbled out into the rain.

Roy stood in the alcove, his head in the garden, holding the door open for the hedgehogs as they walked between his front legs and stumbled outside.

Merry snuffled around the kitchen making sure all the hedgehogs followed Harry. When the last hog left, she barked at Roy.

"That's the lot of them. Now you get out of here too, and I never want to see you in my house again."

Roy drew his head back into the house and looked at Merry. He licked his lips.

"The feeling is mutual, darling. Harry, Cassie, be seeing you."

The fox dived through the cat door and disappeared into the stormy night.

Merry growled and wandered back into the flooded room. Harry was glad to see her go. He hoped he'd never be so close to a dog again in his life.

"Cassie, I've a favour to ask before I leave."

The cat yawned and stretched luxuriantly.

"Well, that was a night I won't soon forget. What is it, little hog?"

Harry waddled closer to Cassie and looked up at her. He knew it was a lot to ask, but after all the horrific experiences he had just been through, he felt he was brave enough to ask her for it.

"Promise me that you won't catch Tina or any of her family and friends, and because you mightn't know which mice might be friends of Tina, you better stop catching mice altogether. It's not like you need to eat them anyway."

Cassie sat down and licked her shoulder for a few moments.

"Are you calling me fat, Harry?"

She purred with laughter, and then stood up and sauntered after Merry into the flooded room. She called back to him over her shoulder.

"I can't promise I won't catch them, but I promise I won't play with them. Unless they want me to."

Harry knew he would have to be satisfied with that. He pushed at the cat door and climbed out into the garden with difficulty. The bodies of the dead hedgehogs on the patio made him sad, but there was nothing more he could do for them.

He forged through the rain, crossing the patio and the lawn. He was tired and wet, but he thought he could do some foraging on the way home and the rain made the ground soft so that it was easy to dig up nice juicy worms. Sometimes they even dug their way out of the ground to greet the rain, saving him the bother of having to dig.

As he passed the compost heap, he heard a soft voice calling his name. He turned around and Tina darted out from the shelter of the shed and pressed close against his shoulder.

"Thank you, Harry. I heard what you said to Cassie. You've saved my life so many times tonight, how can I ever thank you?"

Harry snuffled the ground. He was hungry and his thoughts turned to worms.

"No need to thank me, Tina."

The field mouse pressed her paw against Harry's face.

"You're a good hedgehog. Do you think the poison will come back?"

Harry shook the rain from his body.

"No, the water will wash it away from the field and into the rivers. We'll be safe from now on. I don't think we have to worry about fighting any more zogs."

Tina turned away and moved back towards the shed.

"Zogs. I like that. At least, if there are more, we will know what to do."

Harry grunted, but he wasn't listening. He was following the trail of a slug into the compost heap and he was already salivating at the thought of its delicious, chewy body.

Epilogue

C laire felt the desperate need for coffee. She'd hardly slept a wink last night. Merry had barked constantly, and even the animals in the garden had yelped and squealed into the early hours of the morning. She blamed the oppressive heat, but at least the thunderstorm had broken that. The animals had quietened down after the rain started as well.

She got a shock when she opened her kitchen door and water rushed across her ankles into the hall. The tap was on, looked like it had been on all night, and the dirty dishes she'd left in the sink must have blocked the plug and overflow drain.

Cursing, Claire waded through the water, clinging onto the counters for balance. The water made the tiles so slippery they may as well have been ice.

The water turned off, Claire surveyed the damage. The kitchen stank with a strong animal musk, and she suspected Merry had toileted somewhere, although she couldn't see it. Cassie lay sleeping on top of the table, and Merry, looking rather bedraggled, thumped her tail sleepily from her bed on the other side of the room.

"How am I going to get rid of all this water?"

Claire scratched her head. It was too early in the morning to deal with this, and she hadn't even had her coffee yet.

Her foot nudged against something soggy as she stumbled towards the back door. She thought it was a dog toy at first, but when she looked more closely, she realised it was a dead thing. Some sort of dead animal, and there were more of them too. At least half a dozen dotted around the room.

Claire screamed. She'd have to lock the cat door at night in future. She couldn't put up with Cassie bringing dead things into the house.

Irritation rising, Claire progressed to the back door and flung it open. She screamed again upon seeing the dozens of dead bodies covering her lovely patio area. What exactly had happened last night? Had it rained hedgehogs? She'd have to talk to Jerry about leaving cat food outside to attract hedgehogs to the garden. They seemed to be killing each other to get the tasty treat.

The mud room was a mess as well, with the dog food bag lying near the door and the shoes and coats in a mess. Merry must have tried to eat her way through the plastic. She wasn't normally a greedy dog, but maybe the storm had made her anxious. She'd get Jerry to put it in the shed later, although she was worried mice would get at it there. Maybe she'd get one of those metal containers for it like people had for horse feed.

She picked up the wellington boots and righted them, placing them neatly in a line by the door. She was surprised to see hedgehogs under each boot. There was something wrong with these hedgehogs though. They twitched violently, and their spines were covered in foam. Worst of all, their eyes were a cloudy colour, like they had cataracts.

"What in the..."

The hedgehogs darted towards Claire's bare feet and bit down hard on her toes, drawing blood. It hurt like the blazes, and when she tried to shake them off, she slipped on the tiles and fell hard onto her back.

The hedgehogs gnawed on Claire's toes as she lay vulnerable on her back. As they crunched their way through her left foot, Claire started to twitch and foam at the mouth.

Your Free Book Awaits

Dylan's nightmares are about to become reality.

Sometimes the more things change, the more they stay the same.

Dylan returns home for the funeral of his mother. After decades away, the fears that drove him to flee seem like childish nightmares.

Dylan is about to find out whether it's true what they say. You can never go back.

From the author of the 7th Hell series comes a chilling tale of horror.

About the Author

Iseult Murphy started writing at a young age, entertaining her family with magazines that she wrote and illustrated as a child. In her teens, she won several local and national short story competitions, including being awarded overall winner of the RDS Young Science Writers competition three times, and had work placed in international contests such as the BBC Wildlife Poetry competition.

Iseult is drawn to horror, fantasy and science fiction, as she feels that the most difficult aspects of life can be best explored through the lens of speculative fiction.

She currently resides on the east coast of Ireland. When she isn't writing, she enjoys reading, art and spending time with her animals.